Magical Bedtime Stories

ARCTURUS

ARCTURUS

This edition published in 2012 by Arcturus Publishing Limited
26/27 Bickels Yard, 151–153 Bermondsey Street,
London SE1 3HA

Copyright © 2012 Arcturus Publishing Limited

ISBN: 978-1-84837-866-7
CH001897US
Supplier 13, Date 0212, Print run 1005

Written and designed by Nicola Baxter
Illustrated by Jo Parry and Marie Allen

Printed in China

Contents

Jack and the Beanstalk

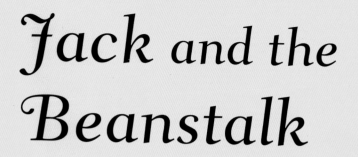

Along time ago, a boy named Jack lived with his mother. They were very poor.

"We will have to sell the cow, Jack," said his mother one day. "Take her to market and get as much for her as you can."

Jack set off along the road with the cow. He wished he did not have to walk all the way to market.

Before he had gone very far, Jack met an old man.

"I can see you are a clever boy," he told Jack, "so listen to me. If you give me your cow, I will give you something much more precious."

"All right," said Jack, without thinking very hard. The old man handed over a small bag.

"In there," he said, "are five magic beans. They are very rare indeed."

Jack couldn't wait to get home with his bargain.

"You did *WHAT*?" yelled his mother when Jack showed her the beans. "You silly boy. There's no such thing as a magic bean."

Angrily, she threw the beans out of the window and sent Jack to bed without dinner.

When Jack woke up the next morning, the room was dark. A huge beanstalk was growing just outside and blocking the window. It had grown from the magic beans!

Jack didn't stop to think about what had happened. He saw that the beanstalk had many, many thick branches, and he was a boy who loved to climb. In a second, he had crawled out of the window and was climbing up the beanstalk as fast as he could.

Jack climbed and climbed. The beanstalk grew up through the clouds. At the top, Jack was amazed to find that he was in another country. Everything seemed very big there. Jack would have wondered about that if he had not been worrying about something much more important.

He had not had dinner last night and now he had missed breakfast. His tummy was rumbling!

Far away across some fields, Jack could see a huge castle. There was sure to be some food there, he thought. He set off toward it.

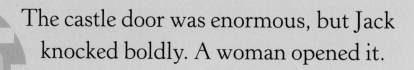

The castle door was enormous, but Jack knocked boldly. A woman opened it.

"Quick! Quick! Come in!" she cried. "If my husband the giant comes home, he'll eat you!"

Jack hurried inside. A moment later he heard a great roar.

Fee-fi-fo-fum, I smell the blood of an Englishman.
Be he alive or be he dead,
I'll grind his bones to make my bread!

"Quick!" cried the woman, and she pushed Jack into the oven to hide. Luckily, it was not hot!

Peering out, Jack saw the giant eating his dinner. When the giant had finished, he began to count gold coins into little bags. At last, he fell asleep.

Quick as a flash, Jack dashed out of the oven, grabbed a bag of coins, and scampered down the beanstalk.

Jack's mother was overjoyed to see the coins. For a few months, all was well, but then the money began to run out. Jack decided to climb the beanstalk again. He headed straight for the castle, where the kind woman opened the door. Just as before, a few moments later the earth began to shake and a voice could be heard roaring:

Fee-fi-fo-fum, I smell the blood of an Englishman.
Be he alive or be he dead,
I'll grind his bones to make my bread!

"Oh no, not again!" cried the woman. "Quick! Hide!"

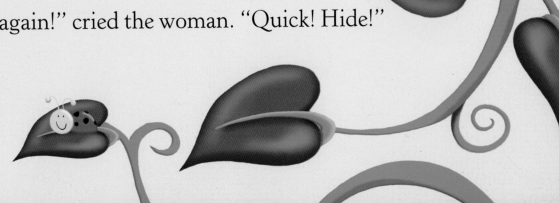

This time, when the giant had eaten, he asked for his golden hen. To Jack's amazement, the hen laid a golden egg! The giant smiled and went to sleep.

Once more, Jack made his escape. Instead of stealing the golden egg, he picked up the hen and ran home as fast as he could.

With a hen that laid a golden egg each day, Jack and his mother had nothing more to worry about. Even so, Jack decided to have one last adventure.

Everything happened just as before, but when the giant had eaten, he called, "Bring me my harp!"

His wife brought a golden harp, which began to play all by itself. At once, the giant fell asleep. Jack grabbed the harp and ran to the door.

"*STOP!*" cried the magic harp.

The giant awoke at once. He stormed after Jack. When Jack reached the beanstalk, he hurled himself down it.

"Mother!" he yelled. "Fetch the ax!"

Jack swung the ax. The huge beanstalk fell, and with it tumbled the giant, never to trouble anyone again. Jack could not climb to magic lands now, but he and his mother lived happily ever after.

Chicken Licken

There was once a little chick called Chicken Licken. One day, as he was scratching about under an old oak tree, an acorn fell on his head. Chicken Licken didn't see the acorn. "*Ouch!*" he cried. "The sky is falling down! I must go tell the King."

Chicken Licken ran through the farmyard, where he met Henny Penny.

"Oh, Henny Penny," cried Chicken Licken, "the sky is falling down and I'm going to tell the King."

"*Cluck! Cluck!* I will come too," said Henny Penny.

Chicken Licken and Henny Penny were just going through the farmyard gate when they met Cocky Locky.

"Oh, Cocky Locky," cried Chicken Licken, "the sky is falling down and we're going to tell the King."

"*Doodle-doo!* I will come too," said Cocky Locky.

Chicken Licken, Henny Penny and Cocky Locky were hurrying past the pond when they met Ducky Lucky.

"Oh, Ducky Lucky," cried Chicken Licken, "the sky is falling down and we're going to tell the King."

"*Quack! Quack!* I will come too," said Ducky Lucky.

Chicken Licken, Henny Penny, Cocky Locky and Ducky Lucky were scurrying along the lane when they met Goosey Loosey.

"Oh, Goosey Loosey," cried Chicken Licken, "the sky is falling down and we're going to tell the King."

"*Honk! Honk!* I will come too," said Goosey Loosey.

Chicken Licken, Henny Penny, Cocky Locky, Ducky Lucky and Goosey Loosey were turning the corner when they met Turkey Lurkey.

"Oh, Turkey Lurkey," cried Chicken Licken, "the sky is falling down and we're going to tell the King."

"*Gobble! Gobble!* I will come too," said Turkey Lurkey.

Chicken Licken, Henny Penny, Cocky Locky, Ducky Lucky, Goosey Loosey and Turkey Lurkey had come to the edge of the forest when they met Foxy Loxy.

"My, my," said Foxy Loxy, "where are you all off to this fine day?"

"Oh, Foxy Loxy," cried Chicken Licken, "the sky is falling down and we're going to tell the King."

"Then come with me," said Foxy Loxy. "I will take you to the King."

So Chicken Licken, Henny Penny, Cocky Locky, Ducky Lucky, Goosey Loosey and Turkey Lurkey followed Foxy Loxy. He took them into the forest, where his family was waiting for dinner.

Poor Chicken Licken, Henny Penny, Cocky Locky, Ducky Lucky, Goosey Loosey and Turkey Lurkey were never seen again.

And the fox family lived happily ever after, although ever so many acorns fell on their heads.

Puss in Boots

Once there was a miller who had three sons. When he died, he left the mill to his eldest son and his donkey to his second son. The third son was not so lucky. All that was left as his share was the family cat.

"I'm sorry, Puss," said the miller's son. "I don't know what we are going to do. How can I even look after you with no job and no money?"

"Don't worry," said the cat. "Just give me some boots and a bag and we'll be fine."

The miller's son was puzzled, but he did as the cat asked. Puss pulled on the boots and filled the bag with lettuce leaves. Then he marched off to a meadow, put down the bag, and sat down to wait.

Just as Puss had planned, before long a little rabbit hopped over to the bag and began to nibble at the lettuce. In a flash, Puss scooped up the bag. Holding it carefully so that the rabbit could not escape, he hurried off to the King's palace.

When he saw the King, Puss swept off his hat and bowed low.

"Your Majesty," he said, "may I present you with this very fine rabbit, a gift from my master, the Marquis of Carrabas?"

The king frowned. "I don't believe I know him," he said, "but you deserve a treat from the palace kitchens."

While he was tucking into a tasty treat, Puss overheard the servants talking. The very next day, the King and his daughter would be taking a drive by the river.

Puss returned to his master. In the morning, he told him, "Go for a swim in the river. If anyone asks, say that your name is the Marquis of Carrabas."

The miller's son did as the cat said. He went to the river, took off his ragged clothes and jumped in. Puss quickly hid the clothes in the bushes. A minute later, the royal carriage drove past, with the King and his daughter the Princess inside.

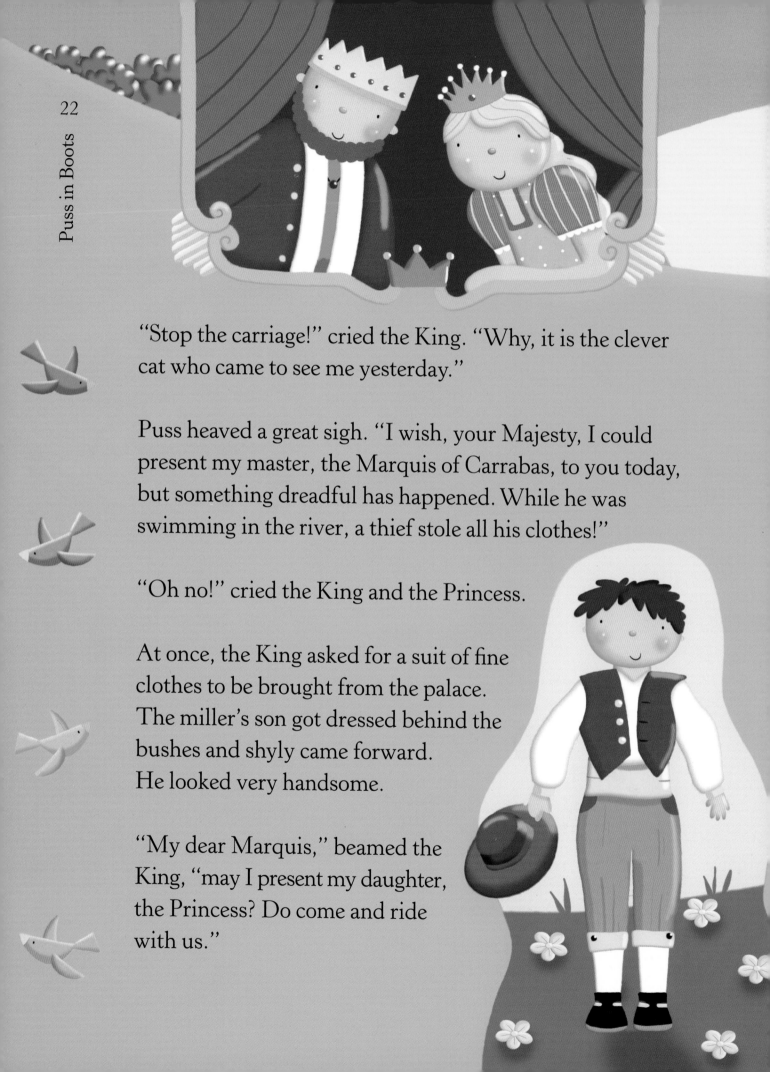

"Stop the carriage!" cried the King. "Why, it is the clever cat who came to see me yesterday."

Puss heaved a great sigh. "I wish, your Majesty, I could present my master, the Marquis of Carrabas, to you today, but something dreadful has happened. While he was swimming in the river, a thief stole all his clothes!"

"Oh no!" cried the King and the Princess.

At once, the King asked for a suit of fine clothes to be brought from the palace. The miller's son got dressed behind the bushes and shyly came forward. He looked very handsome.

"My dear Marquis," beamed the King, "may I present my daughter, the Princess? Do come and ride with us."

Meanwhile, Puss was scampering on ahead. He saw a man making hay in a meadow. "The King will be here in a moment," Puss told him. "My master, the Marquis of Carrabas, will be very grateful if you tell the King that he owns all the land around here."

"I can do that," said the man, "but let's hope the ogre who lives in that castle doesn't hear me. The land is his."

"What a fine hay meadow!" cried the King, when he came along a few minutes later. "Tell me, my man, whose is it?"

"It belongs to the Marquis of Carrabas, your Majesty," the man replied.

While this was happening, Puss had hurried to the ogre's castle. When the huge ogre opened the door, Puss spoke up boldly. "I have heard," he said, "that you are a great magician. Is that true?"

"Come in," replied the ogre, "and I will show you!"

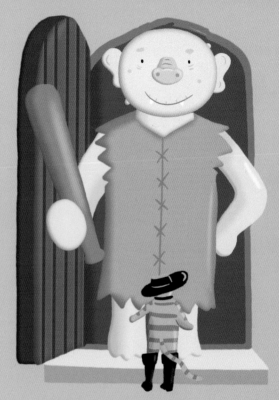

In a flash, he turned himself into a fierce lion.

Puss jumped up on to the furniture.

"Well," he said, "I'm sure it's easy for a big, strong ogre to become a big, strong lion. But could you become a tiny, weak mouse?"

"Just watch me!" roared the ogre. At once, he became
a tiny mouse, scampering across the room.

Puss pounced! He munched up the mouse and looked
around. "This castle is the perfect home for my master,
the Marquis of Carrabas," he said.

When the King saw the castle, he was very impressed.
"The Marquis is just the kind of young man
I should like my daughter to marry,"
he said. The Princess agreed!

So Puss, the Princess and
the miller's son lived
happily ever after.

The Gingerbread Man

*L*ong ago, there lived a little old man and a little old woman in a little old cottage in the country.

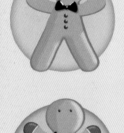

One day, the little old man went to work in the garden, and the little old woman baked some cookies. When she had finished, she had some dough left over, so she made it into a gingerbread man and put him in the oven.

Soon a delicious smell filled the kitchen. The little old woman took the gingerbread man out of the oven and put him on one side to cool. Then she made some frosting. She gave him a black tie, two shiny eyes, three brown buttons, red hands and feet, and a big smile!

The little old woman opened the door to call her husband. Suddenly, the gingerbread man jumped down on to the floor and ran out the door!

"Stop!" cried the little old woman. But the gingerbread man just laughed and began to sing a little song, "Run, run, as fast as you can! You can't catch me, I'm the gingerbread man!"

He ran past the little old man, through the gate and off down the road. The little old man shouted, "Hey! Come back!"

But the gingerbread man ran on. "Run, run, as fast as you can! You can't catch me, I'm the gingerbread man!" he sang, as the little old woman and the little old man ran after him.

Before long, the gingerbread man passed a cow in a field.

"Yoooou look tasty," mooed the cow. She set off after the gingerbread man, the little old woman and the little old man.

The gingerbread man just laughed. "Run, run, as fast as you can!" he sang. "You can't catch me, I'm the gingerbread man!"

A horse heard the song and raised her head.

"I saaaaaay," she neighed, "you look good to eat!" She galloped off down the road after the gingerbread man, the little old woman, the little old man and the cow.

"Ha ha!" sang the gingerbread man. "Run, run, as fast as you can! You can't catch me, I'm the gingerbread man!"

A rooster saw the gingerbread man run past.

"I love cookies," he crowed. "Yes, I cock-a-doodle-doooo!"

He flapped off after the gingerbread man, the little old woman, the little old man, the cow and the horse.

"Ho, ho!" chortled the gingerbread man. "Run, run, as fast as you can! You can't catch me, I'm the gingerbread man!"

"Oink! Oink!" snuffled a sleepy pig. "I smell dinner!" He set off, as fast as his little pink trotters would carry him, after the gingerbread man, the little old woman, the little old man, the cow, the horse and the rooster.

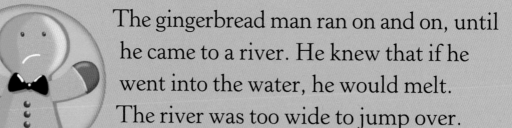

The gingerbread man ran on and on, until he came to a river. He knew that if he went into the water, he would melt. The river was too wide to jump over. He looked around. The little old woman, the little old man, the cow, the horse, the rooster and the pig were getting nearer and nearer.

"Can I help at all?" asked a soft voice. Sitting on the bank was a big, red fox. "Why don't you jump on my back?" he said. "I'll carry you across."

The gingerbread man jumped on at once. He didn't want to be eaten by the little old woman, the little old man, the cow, the horse, the rooster *or* the pig. The fox slid into the water.

"My toes!" cried the gingerbread man, feeling a tiny splash.

"Climb on to my head," said the fox. "You'll be safe there."

Now they were in the middle of the river, where the water was deeper. It almost reached the gingerbread man's feet.

"We're nearly there," said the fox. "Just perch on my nose."

So the gingerbread man climbed on to the fox's nose, but as soon as he did so, the fox tossed him up into the air! The gingerbread man flew up, up, up and then down, down, down … right into the fox's open mouth!

When the little old woman, the little old man, the cow, the horse, the rooster and the pig reached the river, the fox was already on the other side. He was smiling.

And there was no sign at all of the gingerbread man.

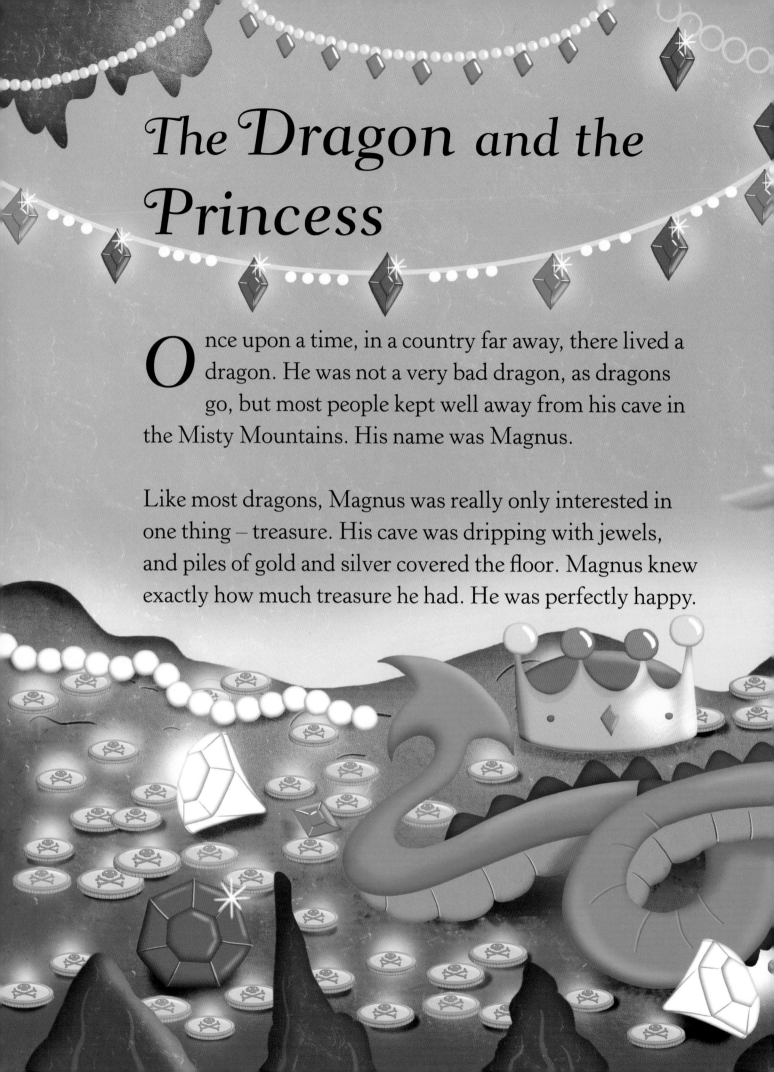

The Dragon and the Princess

Once upon a time, in a country far away, there lived a dragon. He was not a very bad dragon, as dragons go, but most people kept well away from his cave in the Misty Mountains. His name was Magnus.

Like most dragons, Magnus was really only interested in one thing – treasure. His cave was dripping with jewels, and piles of gold and silver covered the floor. Magnus knew exactly how much treasure he had. He was perfectly happy.

One day in spring, Magnus came out of his cave to stretch his wings. He flew around the mountain peaks and enjoyed himself trying out some dragon acrobatics.

He was just finishing a wobbly loop-the-loop when he noticed something. Far below, a procession of people and animals was slowly making its way along a narrow mountain path, led by a girl wearing a crown and riding a white horse.

As soon as he saw the group, Magnus began to wonder if they might be carrying gold and jewels. The glint of the girl's crown caught his eye. Here was a chance to add to his treasure store.

With what he hoped was a terrifying roar, Magnus flew down and landed just in front of the visitors. He saw at once that the girl in front was wearing royal robes and was probably a Princess. Her first words showed he was right.

"I am Princess Merlina!" she said. "And you are in my way!"

Magnus frowned. No one talks to a dragon like that! He took a deep breath and blew scary flames from his nostrils.

The Princess didn't seem frightened, but her horse reared up. Although the Princess clung on, her crown slipped off her head and hurtled down into the deep valley below, twinkling and shining as it fell.

Magnus couldn't help it. He forgot about trying to frighten the Princess and peered down to see where the sparkly treasure had fallen. Merlina scrambled from her horse.

The Princess and the dragon had exactly the same thought at exactly the same moment: *I must get that crown!*

All Magnus had to do was swoop down, seize the crown, and fly away with it. The Princess interrupted his thoughts. "Thank goodness!" she cried. "That's only my travel crown. My two most precious crowns are in my jewel chest. Please, please, take that crown if you must, but don't take my jewel chest!"

Magnus spread his wings and snorted a few more flames to show he meant business. The Princess sighed and beckoned two servants. They staggered forward, each holding one handle of a huge chest.

Completely forgetting about the crown below, Magnus seized the chest with the claws of his scaly feet. Only the thought of the gold and jewels inside gave him the strength to lift it, and it was not until sunset that he reached his cave.

Meanwhile, the Princess sent her page boy to clamber down and rescue her crown, and the royal party left the Misty Mountains with all possible speed.

That night, Magnus snapped the lock of the chest and opened it to find … a picnic! For a moment, he was furious, but not for long. It was a royal picnic after all, and even jewels don't stop a dragon's tummy from rumbling!

Goldilocks
and the Three Bears

Once upon a time, there was a family of bears who
lived in a cottage in a forest. Father Bear had a deep,
growly voice, Mother Bear had a warm, soft voice,
and Baby Bear had a high, squeaky voice.

One morning, before breakfast, the bears went out for a walk.

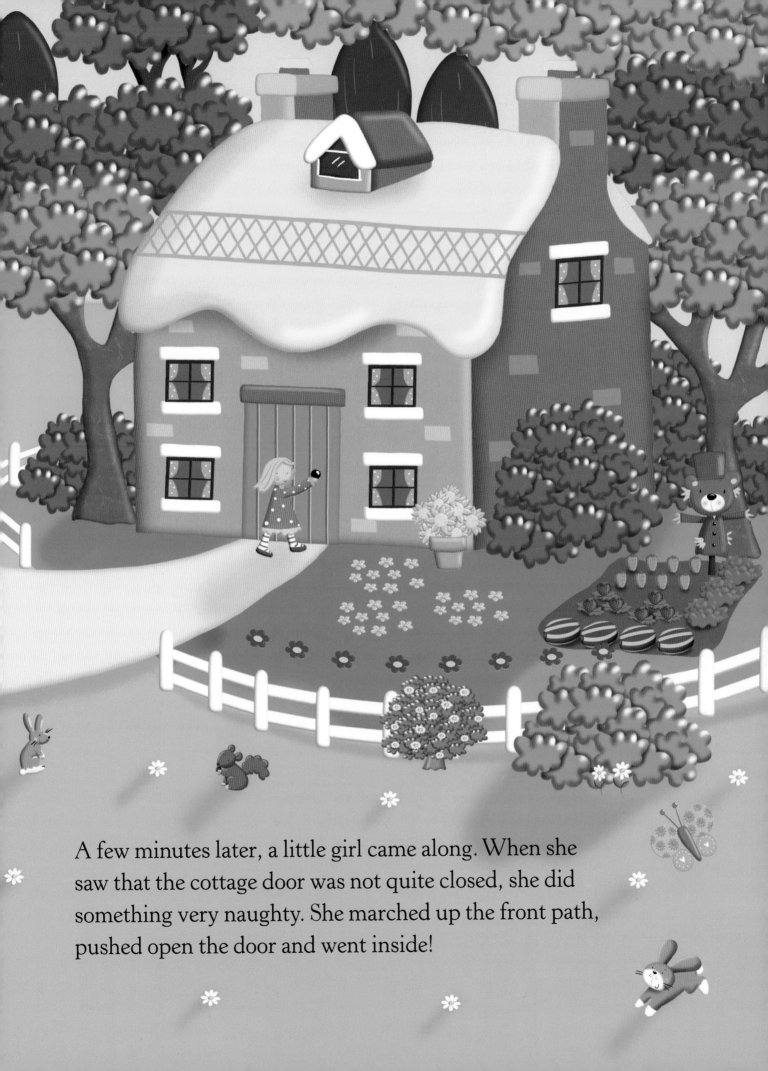

A few minutes later, a little girl came along. When she saw that the cottage door was not quite closed, she did something very naughty. She marched up the front path, pushed open the door and went inside!

The little girl's name was Goldilocks, because she had bright yellow hair. After her walk in the woods, Goldilocks was hungry, so she looked around for something to eat.

On the kitchen table, she spotted three bowls of porridge. She went straight to the biggest bowl, picked up Father Bear's large spoon, and took a mouthful.

"Ouch!" cried Goldilocks. "Much too hot!"

She picked up Mother Bear's medium-sized spoon and tasted *her* porridge.

"*Eeeeeeuuuuw!* Much too sweet!" she said.

Last of all, she tried Baby Bear's porridge. Now Goldilocks didn't say a word. She was much too busy eating!

When she was full, Goldilocks wandered into the living room. She looked around for a comfy chair. She saw three chairs – one large, one medium-sized and one tiny.

Goldilocks climbed on to the huge armchair in the corner. Ow! It was much too hard.

She leapt down and went over to the middle-sized chair. Goldilocks hauled herself up and nearly disappeared! The chair was so soft, she almost sank beneath the cushions.

Goldilocks scrambled out and headed for the smallest chair of all. It looked perfect. She plonked herself down on it.

CRAAAAACK!

BUMP!

OUCH!

Suddenly, Goldilocks felt very tired. She spotted some stairs in the corner of the room and went over to them.

At the top of the stairs was a bedroom with three beds. Goldilocks tested the largest bed.

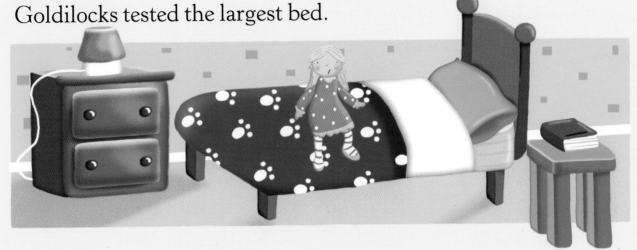

"Ouch! Too hard again!" she cried.

She jumped on to the middle-sized bed.

"Ooof! Too soft!" she groaned.

The smallest bed stood under the window. Goldilocks lay down. Aaah! Perfect! In a second, she was fast asleep.

While Goldilocks slept upstairs, the three bears came back from their walk. Immediately, Father Bear saw that something was wrong.

"Someone's been eating my porridge!" he growled.

"And someone's been eating my porridge!" said Mother Bear.

"And someone's been eating my porridge," cried Baby Bear, "and they've eaten it all up!"

Father Bear strode into the living room.

"Someone's been sitting in my chair!" he muttered.

"Someone's been sitting in my chair, too," said Mother Bear.

"Oooh!" wailed Baby Bear. "Someone's been sitting in my chair – and it's all broken!"

From upstairs there came a tiny snoring sound. The bears crept up the stairs and into the bedroom.

"Someone's been lying on my bed," said Father Bear.

"And someone's been lying on my bed," said Mother Bear.

"And someone's been lying on my bed," squeaked Baby Bear, "and she's still there!"

Just then, Goldilocks woke up and saw the three bears. She gave a little scream, climbed quickly out of the window and ran home as fast as she could. The bears never saw her again.

The Magic Porridge Pot

O nce upon a time, there was a little girl who lived with her mother. They were so poor that sometimes they had no food to eat.

One day, the little girl went into the forest to see if she could find any nuts or berries. She was so hungry and weak, she sat down on a tree stump and began to cry.

"My dear, what is the matter?" asked a kindly voice. An old lady was smiling down at her. "Don't worry," said the stranger kindly, when she heard the little girl's story, "take this pot. It is magic. When you want to eat, simply say, 'Little pot, little pot, porridge, please!' When you want it to stop, say, 'Little pot, little pot, stop now, please!'"

The little girl was not sure she believed in magic, but she took the pot and hurried home.

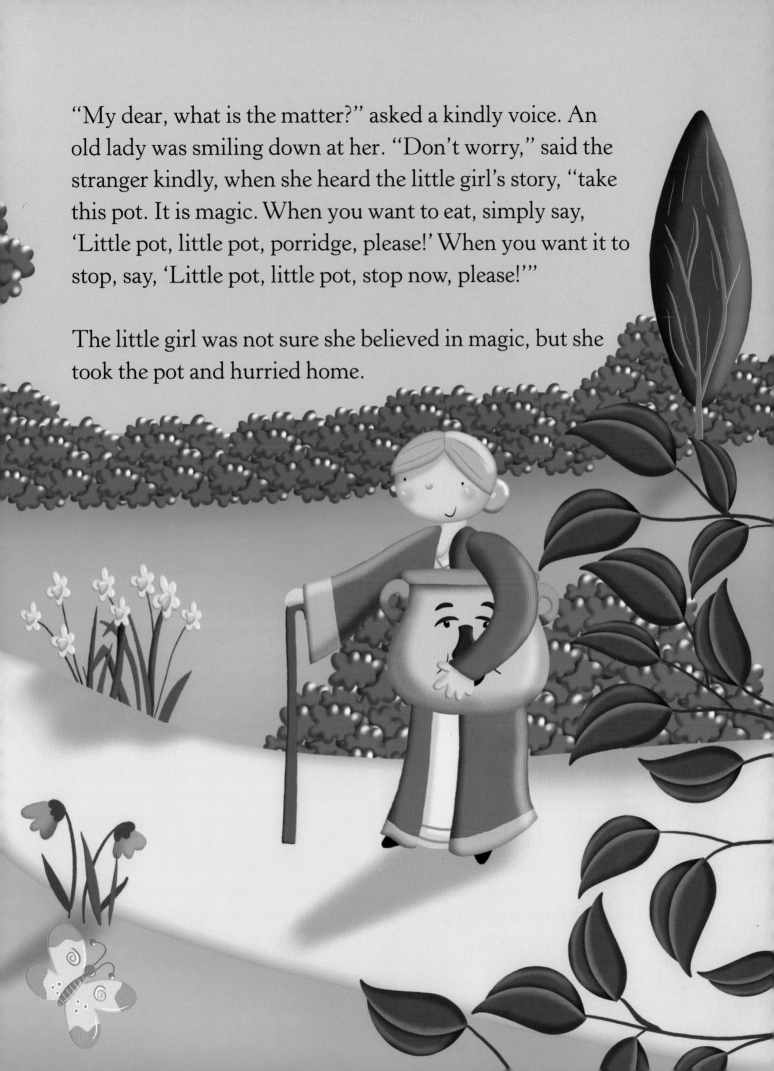

When the little girl explained about the pot, her mother looked doubtful, but said, "There is no harm in trying."

"Little pot, little pot, porridge, please!" said the little girl.

At once, the magic porridge pot became warm and began to jiggle. In a few minutes, the smell of good, hot porridge filled the room. The pot was full to the brim of the most delicious porridge the little girl had ever eaten.

"Little pot, little pot, stop, please," said the girl.

For the first time in ages, she and her mother went to bed with full tummies and smiles on their faces.

The next morning, the same thing happened. "We don't need to worry now," said the mother.

After that, each day, the little girl asked the pot for porridge. She had been hungry for so long, that eating porridge at every meal did not seem bad at all.

One day, the little girl walked to a town a few miles away to visit her aunt. Near lunchtime, her mother began to feel hungry. She wondered if the porridge pot would work if *she* said the magic words.

"Little pot, little pot, porridge, please!" she said. To her delight, she was soon sitting down to a big bowl of hot, tasty porridge.

Just as she was finishing, she noticed that the porridge pot was still cooking. In fact, some porridge had begun to overflow the pot.

"My goodness, I must stop it!" cried the mother. She tried to remember the words that her daughter had said.

"Little pot, little pot, no more porridge, please!" she said, but the pot kept overflowing, oozing across the table.

"Little pot, little pot, that's enough porridge!" she shouted. Porridge began to pour on to the floor.

"Little pot, little pot, stop, please, stop!" cried the mother desperately. It was no good. Porridge was now flowing across the floor and out the door!

That afternoon, the little girl returned from visiting her aunt. As she drew near the village where she lived, she heard shouting and wailing. Whatever could be the matter?

As she reached the main street, the little girl stood still, her mouth open in surprise. The street was knee-deep in porridge! The gloopy, sticky stuff was oozing through doors and out of windows as it filled up the houses. She understood at once what must have happened.

"Help!" came a familiar voice. Leaning out of an attic window, as the house was filling with porridge from bottom to top, clutching the magic porridge pot, was her mother.

The porridge was up to the little girl's waist as she waded to the house. She yelled as loudly as she could, "Little pot, little pot, stop now, please!"

At once, the pot stopped overflowing with porridge.

"Thank goodness!" cried her mother.

As you can imagine, cleaning up the village took a very long time. Farmers herded their cows along the street to help eat it up. Birds fluttered down to peck at the gooey mess. And little animals crept out of the woods to try it, too.

When everywhere was clean again, the little girl and her mother sat down, exhausted.

"It's time for supper," said the mother. "Would you like some porridge?" She began to laugh, and her daughter laughed, too. The porridge was so delicious that even now, they couldn't wait to eat some.

"Just one thing," giggled the little girl.
"I'll do the cooking in future!"

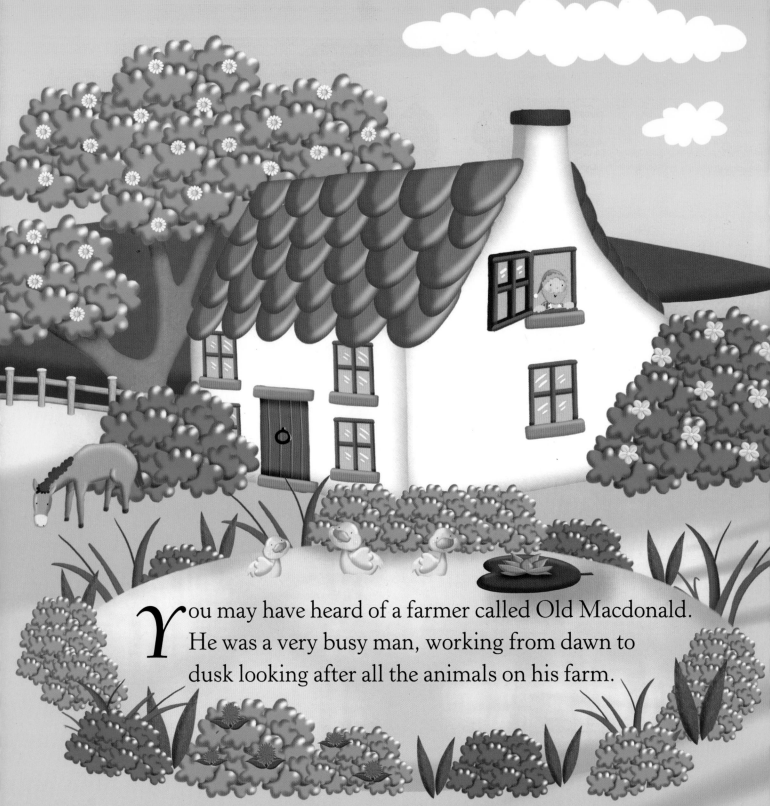

Old Macdonald's Bedtime

You may have heard of a farmer called Old Macdonald. He was a very busy man, working from dawn to dusk looking after all the animals on his farm.

Old Macdonald had no trouble getting up in the morning. As the sun chased the last stars from the sky, Rufus the rooster would flap up on to the farmhouse fence, open his beak wide, and call:

Cock-a-doodle-doooo!

Going to bed was another matter. Old Macdonald found that very difficult. There was so much work to do, he never wanted to stop when it was time to sleep. The animals on the farm began to worry.

"It's not good for him," snuffled Pickle the pig to his duck friends. "He's always yawning. Our farmer needs more sleep."

Doris the duck agreed. "He needs someone to tell him when it's time to go to bed," she quacked.

"Well, Rufus tells Old Macdonald when to get up," said Sam the sheep, "with a big, loud noise like an alarm clock. We could try making a soft sound to send him to sleep."

"We can sing him a lullaby," neighed Harriet the horse. "I know just the right one. We'll need to practice – especially you, Pickle. We don't want any snuffling, snorting or snoring in our song."

"I don't snore!" protested Pickle, but he promised to practice very hard all the same.

All day long, wherever Old Macdonald went on the farm, he heard weird sounds. He noticed that the animals were behaving strangely.

The hens were squawking squeakily. Pickle was oinking instead of eating his dinner.

That night, Old Macdonald was working late as usual.
He was mending his old tractor in the barn.

One by one, as quietly as they could, the animals flapped
and trotted across to the open barn door.
Old Macdonald yawned and rubbed
his eyes. The animals nodded.
It was time for action.

"Ready, everyone?" whispered Doris.
"One, two, three, four...."

Very, very softly and very, very slowly, the animals sang:

Old Macdonald, time for bed!
EE–I–EE–I–O!
Time to rest your sleepy head!
EE–I–EE–I–O!
With a neigh, neigh here,
And a snuffle, snuffle there,
Here a quack, there a baa,
Everywhere a moo, moo.
Old Macdonald, time for bed!
EEEE–I–EEEE–I–OOOOOOOOO!

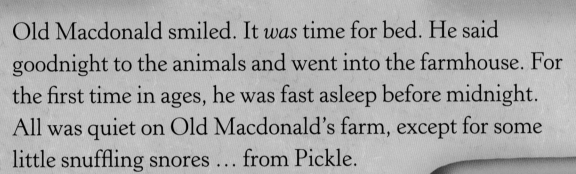

Old Macdonald smiled. It *was* time for bed. He said goodnight to the animals and went into the farmhouse. For the first time in ages, he was fast asleep before midnight. All was quiet on Old Macdonald's farm, except for some little snuffling snores … from Pickle.

The Three Little Pigs

O nce upon a time, there were three little pigs who lived with their mother. The day came when they decided they were big enough and brave enough to set out to find homes of their own.

Mother Pig waved them goodbye. "Remember," she called, as the three little pigs set off down the road, "to look out for the Big, Bad Wolf."

"We will!" replied the little pigs.

It wasn't long before they met a man with a load of straw.

"I could build a very good house with that straw," said the first little pig. He bought the straw and said goodbye to his brother and sister, who walked on down the road.

The first little pig worked hard. By dinnertime, he had built himself a very snug little house.

The first little pig had only just gone inside when he heard a knock at the door. He peeped through the window and saw that his visitor was none other than the Big, Bad Wolf!

"Little pig, little pig, let me come in!" called the wolf in his sweetest voice (which was not very sweet at all).

The first little pig tried to sound bold and brave. "No, no, by the hair on my chinny chin chin, I will *not* let you in!"

"Then I'll huff and I'll puff and I'll blow your house down!" growled the wolf.

The Big, Bad Wolf took a deep breath. He *huffed* and he *puffed* and he blew the house down! The first little pig ran off as fast as his trotters could carry him.

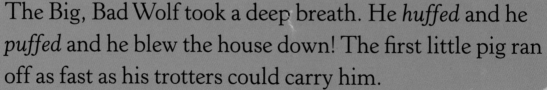

Meanwhile, the second and third little pigs had walked on down the winding road. Soon they met a man with a load of sticks.

"I could make myself a very good house with those sticks," said the second little pig.

He bought all the sticks, waved goodbye to his sister, and set to work. Before long, he had built a snug little house.

The second little pig was just settling down for the night when there came a knock at the door. It was the first little pig!

"Let me in!" he cried. "The Big, Bad Wolf is close behind me!"

No sooner was the little pig safe inside than there came a fierce shout: "Little pigs, little pigs, let me come in!"

"No, no, by the hair on our chinny chin chins," replied the two little pigs, "we will *not* let you in!"

"Then I'll huff and I'll puff and I'll blow your house down!"

The Big, Bad Wolf took a deep breath and he *huffed* …

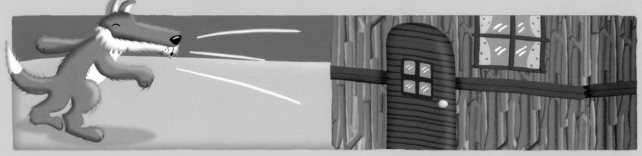

and he *puffed* …

and he blew the house down!

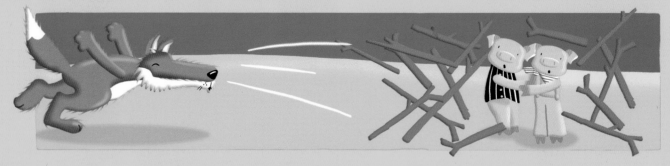

It was hard work. While the Big, Bad Wolf was too out of breath to run, the two little pigs scuttled off down the road to find their sister.

She had also spent a busy day. Soon after saying goodbye to her brother, she had met a man with a cart full of bricks.

"With those bricks, I could make a beautiful house," she said. She bought the whole load and set to work. Before the moon had risen in the sky, she was sitting before her own fire, feeling warm and safe.

Suddenly, there came a hammering at the door. "Let us in, let us in!" cried her brothers. "The Big, Bad Wolf is on his way!"

"We'll see about that!" said the third little pig. She let her brothers in and locked the door.

It wasn't long before they heard the wolf outside. "Little pigs, little pigs, let me come in!"

"No, no, by the hair on our chinny chin chins," chorused the three little pigs, "we will *not* let you in!"

"Then I'll huff and I'll puff and I'll blow your house down!" fumed the wolf.

He *huffed* and he *puffed*. The brick house stood strong and true. The wolf tried again. He *huffed* and he *puffed* and he *puffed* and he *huffed*! But it was no good.

Now the wolf was really angry. He couldn't blow the house down. The door was locked and the windows were closed.

Then he had an idea.

"He's trying to climb down the chimney!" whispered the girl pig. "Help me with this pot!"

The pigs dragged a huge pot on to the fire and filled it with water. By the time the wolf had squeezed himself down the chimney, the pot was boiling merrily. The wolf landed in the fireplace and scalded his tail in the boiling water.

"*Yeeeeeeeeeeowwwww!*" he yelled. That Big, Bad Wolf shot straight up the chimney and off down the road. He was never seen again, and the three little pigs lived happily ever after.

The Perfect Pirate

O nce upon a time, a pirate family lived in a tumbledown cottage near the sea. They were Pa Pirate, Ma Pirate and little Petey Pirate.

Ma and Pa Pirate were feared from one shore of the Swirly Sea to the other. They hoped that little Petey would grow up to be a perfect pirate, too. When he was only a baby, they began to teach him pirate ways.

"Say 'Aaaaaaaarrrgh!' Petey," begged Ma Pirate.

"Doo doo, da da!" cooed little Petey.

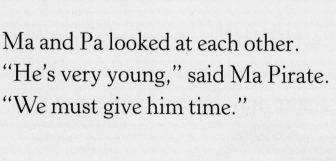

Ma and Pa looked at each other. "He's very young," said Ma Pirate. "We must give him time."

But as little Petey grew, he didn't become more fearsome. He was a well-mannered child, always smiling. Ma and Pa were upset that their beloved son seemed far too polite to be a proper pirate.

"Petey, how many times do I have to tell you?" his father would say. "You don't put your goblet away on the shelf like that. Hurl it on the floor like this!"

"But that makes a mess," said Petey.

As he grew up, Petey loved reading, nature, drawing, music and dancing. He showed no interest at all in fighting, swearing, or going to bed with his seaboots on.

Ma and Pa Pirate had a serious talk.

"There's only one thing to do," said Pa Pirate. "We must take him on a voyage. The boy has pirate blood. When he's on the deck of a ship, with a fierce sou'westerly blowing in his ears, he'll know he is a pirate."

"I agree," said Ma. "We'll take Old Bartholomew's treasure map with us and look for his buried booty."

"I've never been able to make head nor tail of that map," confessed Pa Pirate, "but we can have another go."

So Ma and Pa Pirate packed up their belongings (well, other people's belongings really), cleaned their cutlasses, and stowed everything away on board their ship, the *Seahorse*.

The pirate parents loved being at sea again. They stomped around the deck, crying, "Avast me hearties!" and "Sluice me scuppers!" Petey curled up on the deck, looking pale.

After a few days, Petey stopped feeling seasick and took an interest – in studying shipworms and drawing clouds.

"It's no good," sighed Pa. "I'm sorry to say it, but our boy will never be a proper pirate. He can't do even the simplest dastardly deed, and our parrot would be more use in a fight."

"Never mind," said Ma Pirate, "let's cheer ourselves up by looking for Old Bartholomew's treasure. Now, where's that map?"

It was the parrot who found the map in the end. Unfortunately, Ma and Pa Pirate hadn't one idea in their noddles about map-reading. They had spent many happy years searching for hidden treasure, but they had never found so much as a single doubloon.

Ma and Pa looked at the treasure map, scratching their heads. At last, Pa swung the ship's wheel around toward the east. Young Petey Pirate took a break from worm study and went over to see what they were doing.

"You've got the map the wrong way up," Petey told his mother. "And you're going in the wrong direction," he said to his father.

"How do you know?" spluttered Pa Pirate.

Petey explained. He used words that Ma and Pa had never heard of, such as latitude, longitude and longshore drift.

Ma and Pa looked at each other. They knew their chance of finding the treasure was very small. Following Petey's advice couldn't make things worse.

"All right, son," said Pa Pirate. "I'll give you a week."

Petey Pirate didn't need a week. Two days later, the Pirate family was sitting on the beach of a tiny island. The Pirate parents gazed open-mouthed at the cascade of sparkling jewels tumbling from Old Bartholomew's sea chest.

"I don't believe it!" gasped Pa Pirate. "We're rich!"
Ma Pirate gave Petey a hug. "Our Petey may not be
fearsome, or quick with a cutlass," she said, "but he's the
best treasure-finder in all of the Swirly Sea, and *that*
means he is a *perfect* pirate."

The Little Red Hen

There was once a little red hen who lived with her friends on a farm. One day, the little red hen found some ears of wheat that had fallen from the farmer's truck. She didn't eat them at once, for as soon as she saw them, she had an idea.

"Who will help me plant this wheat?" she asked her friends.

"Well, I won't," said the cat.

"Nor will I," said the rat.

"I simply can't," said the pig.

"Then I'll do it myself," said the little red hen. And she did.

The tiny grains of wheat grew little green shoots, then strong, tall stems. At the top, ears of wheat slowly ripened in the sun. At last, the little red hen saw that the wheat was ready to be cut.

"Who will help me harvest the wheat?" she asked.

"Well, I won't," said the cat.

"Nor will I," said the rat.

"I simply can't," said the pig.

"Then I'll do it myself," said the little red hen. And she did.

When she had cut all the wheat and put it in a sack, the little red hen went to her friends again.

"Who will help me take the wheat to the mill to be ground into flour?" she asked.

"Well, I won't," said the cat.

"Nor will I," said the rat.

"I simply can't," said the pig.

"Then I'll do it myself," said the little red hen. And she did.

When the miller had ground the wheat into flour, the little red hen took it back to the farm.

FLOUR

"Who will help me make some bread with this flour?"
she asked her friends.

"Well, I won't," said the cat.

"Nor will I," said the rat.

"I simply can't," said the pig.

"Then I'll do it myself," said the little red hen. And she did.

Soon a wonderful smell came from the farmhouse kitchen.
The bread was ready!

The little red hen appeared at the farmhouse door. She called to her friends, who were relaxing in the sunshine.

"Who will help me to eat my delicious bread?" called the little red hen.

"Well, I will!" said the cat.

"So will I!" said the rat.

"I simply can't wait!" said the pig.

The little red hen saw that the cat and the rat and the pig were not really friends at all.

"No," she said, "I think I'll eat it myself." And she did.

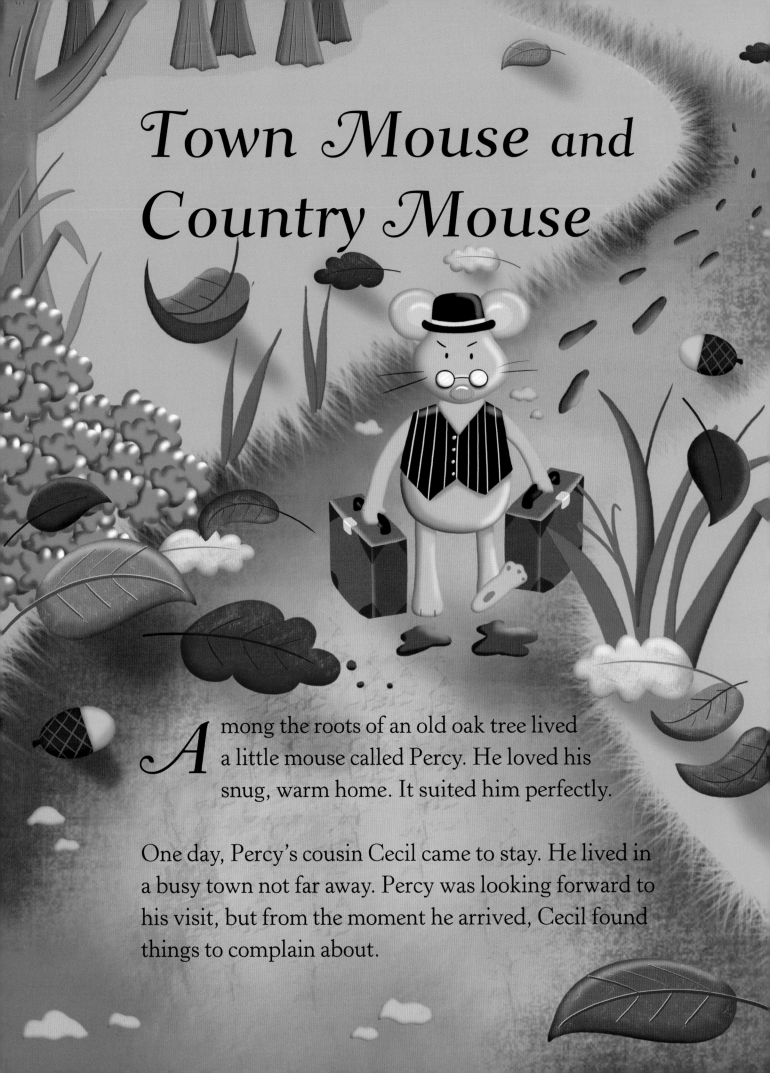

Town Mouse and Country Mouse

A mong the roots of an old oak tree lived a little mouse called Percy. He loved his snug, warm home. It suited him perfectly.

One day, Percy's cousin Cecil came to stay. He lived in a busy town not far away. Percy was looking forward to his visit, but from the moment he arrived, Cecil found things to complain about.

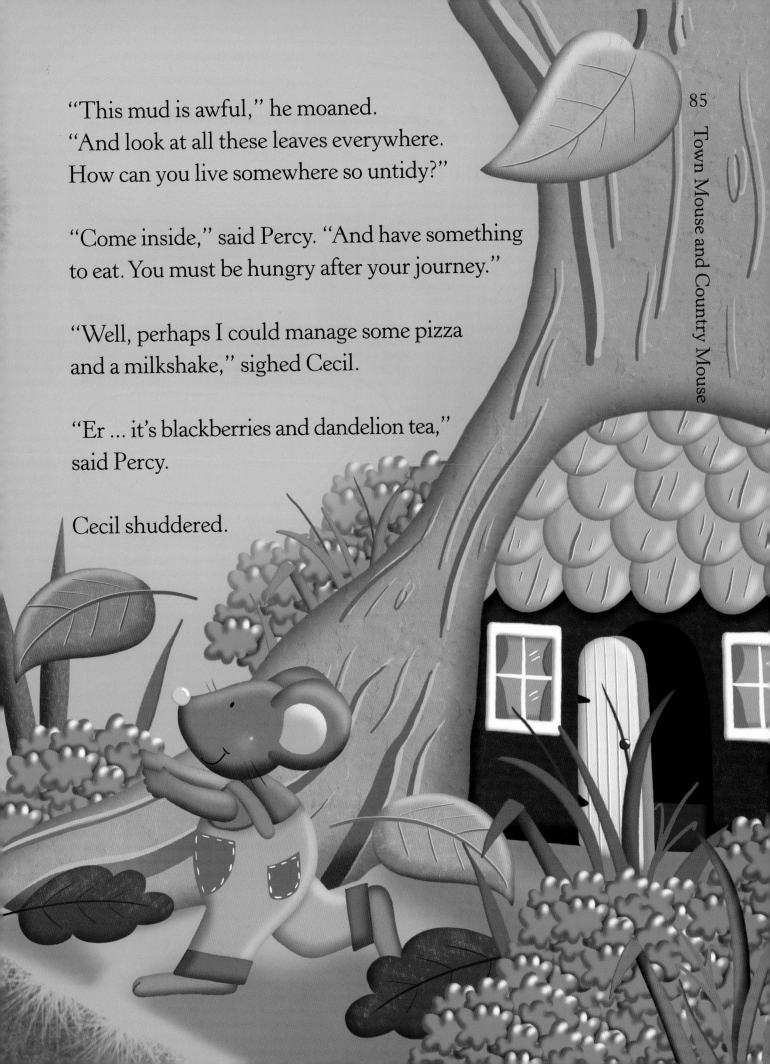

"This mud is awful," he moaned.
"And look at all these leaves everywhere.
How can you live somewhere so untidy?"

"Come inside," said Percy. "And have something
to eat. You must be hungry after your journey."

"Well, perhaps I could manage some pizza
and a milkshake," sighed Cecil.

"Er ... it's blackberries and dandelion tea,"
said Percy.

Cecil shuddered.

Later, when it was dark, Percy gave Cecil a candle and led him to his room. Cecil didn't like the way the candle made flickering, spooky shadows.

"Haven't you heard of electricity?" he asked.

In the middle of the night, Percy was woken by a shriek. He hurried to his cousin.

"This house is haunted! There's a terrible creaking, moaning sound," sobbed Cecil.

"I can't hear anything," a puzzled Percy replied. Then he smiled. "It's just my old tree swaying in the wind," he said. "It's a lovely sound."

Next morning, Cecil complained that he had hardly slept at all.

"Let's go for a walk," Percy said.

It wasn't a great success. Cecil complained about long grass, insects and the cold. On the way home, Cecil suddenly shouted, "HELP! There's a monster behind the hedge!"

Percy peeped through the bushes. "It's a cow," he said. "You're not enjoying yourself, are you, Cecil?"

"I'm sorry, Percy," Cecil replied, "this is not the place for me. I'm going back to town this afternoon. Why don't you come with me? You'll wonder why you lived here so long."

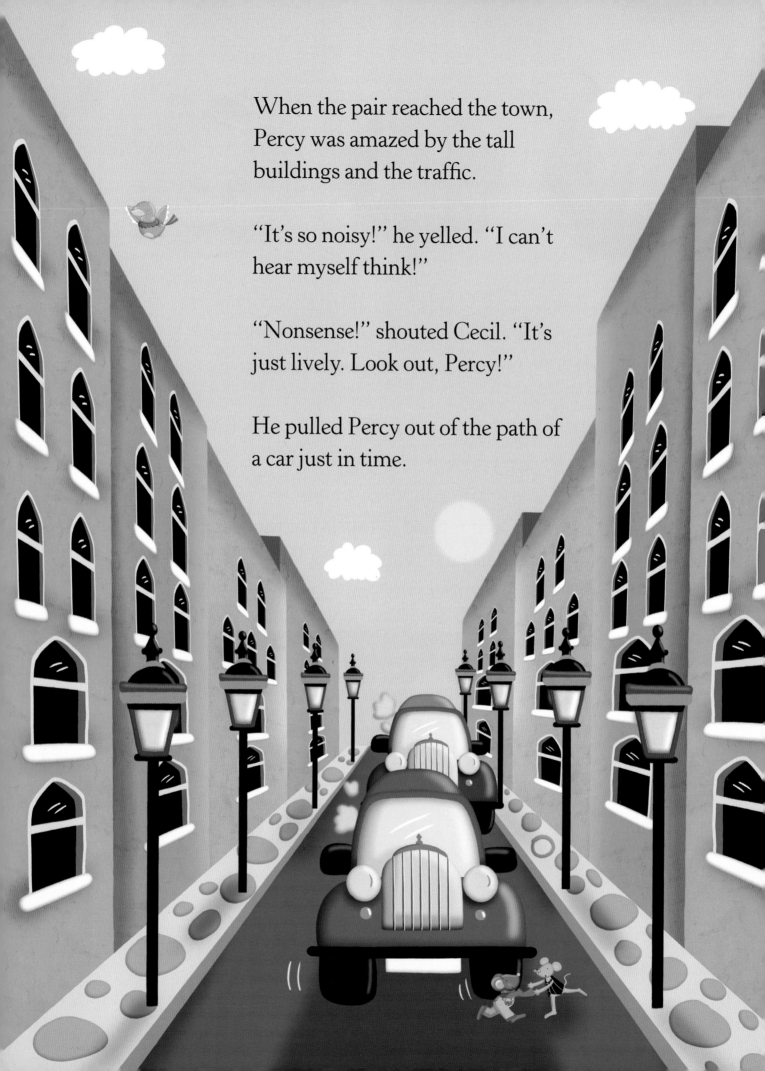

When the pair reached the town, Percy was amazed by the tall buildings and the traffic.

"It's so noisy!" he yelled. "I can't hear myself think!"

"Nonsense!" shouted Cecil. "It's just lively. Look out, Percy!"

He pulled Percy out of the path of a car just in time.

Cecil's home was behind the walls of a grand house. He proudly showed Percy his electric light, his running water, and his heating system.

"You don't have a kitchen," said Percy.

"No need!" smiled Cecil. "There's always plenty of food."

Cecil took Percy to the pantry of the house and scampered up on to the shelves."What will you have, Percy?" he asked. "Apple pie? Custard? Cake? A little cheese?"

Percy was not used to such rich food. He could only eat a little.

As they strolled back down a long, carpeted corridor, Cecil suddenly squeaked, "Quick! Run for your life! This way!"

He set off at an incredible pace, with Percy panting behind.

"What is it?" cried Percy as they scurried into Cecil's home.

"C-c-c-c-cat!" stammered Cecil.

"But how did she get in?" asked Percy.

"She didn't," replied Cecil. "She lives here, too. I have to watch out for her *all the time*."

Hole ❀
❀ *Sweet Hole*

Percy didn't sleep well that night. Dreams of thundering traffic and prowling cats made him restless. The next morning he packed his bag.

"It's been … interesting," he told Cecil, "but I feel more comfortable in my home, just as you feel more comfortable in yours."

That night, safe in his own little house, Percy sat down to write to his cousin. "Visiting is fun," he wrote, "but there really is no place like home."

The Three Billy Goats Gruff

High in the mountains, there lived three billy goats called Gruff. One day, they set off to find some sweet, green grass to eat. They trotted down the mountainside until they came to a valley with a river running through it. On the other side of the river was a meadow of the sweetest, greenest grass they had ever seen.

There was a rickety wooden bridge over the river, but the billy goats Gruff knew that under the bridge lived an ugly old troll. Whenever he heard footsteps overhead, he would leap out and gobble up anyone who dared try to cross.

The three billy goats Gruff wondered what to do. Then the smallest billy goat had an idea and set off toward the river. *Trip, trap, trip, trap,* went his hoofs on the wooden bridge.

At once, the troll jumped out from underneath. "Who's that trip-trapping over my bridge?" he roared.

The smallest billy goat Gruff trembled. "It's me," he said, "I'm off to the meadow to eat the sweet, green grass."

"Oh no, you're not," bellowed the troll. "I'm going to eat you up!"

"Please don't!" cried the smallest billy goat. "My brother is coming along next. He's much fatter and tastier than me."

"Off you go then!" yelled the troll. "I can wait."

The smallest billy goat Gruff trotted off into the meadow and began to eat the sweet, green grass. A minute later, the second billy goat Gruff's hoofs could be heard going *trip, trap, trip, trap,* across the wooden bridge.

Once again, the troll jumped out. "Who's that trip-trapping over my bridge?" he roared.

The second billy goat Gruff replied boldly. "It's me," he said, "I'm off to the meadow to eat the sweet, green grass."

"Oh no, you're not," bellowed the troll. "I'm going to eat you!"

"Don't!" cried the second billy goat. "My big brother will be here soon. He'll be much tastier!"

"All right!" the troll yelled. "Go on your way!"

The second billy goat Gruff galloped off into the meadow to join his little brother and eat the sweet, green grass. At last, the biggest billy goat Gruff set off across the bridge. *TRIP, TRAP, TRIP, TRAP,* went his mighty hoofs.

The troll jumped out from under the bridge. "I've been waiting for you!" he roared. "I'm going to eat you up!"

"Oh, no you're not!" bellowed the biggest billy goat.

TRIP, TRAP, TRIP, TRAP, the biggest billy goat Gruff thundered across the bridge. He lowered his head and butted the troll with his huge horns. *BOOMF!* The troll flew up into the air and down into the river. *SPLASH!*

The three billy goats Gruff ate the sweet, green grass and grew bigger every day. The troll was never seen again.

The Golden Goose

Once a woodcutter and his wife had three sons. They loved the two older boys, but for some reason they only ever made fun of the youngest.

One day, the eldest boy went into the forest to chop some wood. His mother gave him some cakes and milk for his lunch. To his surprise, when he sat down to eat and drink, a little man appeared beside him.

"I'm hungry and thirsty," said the little man.
"Could I have a cake and some milk?"

"Of course not!" laughed the eldest son.
"I won't have enough for myself if you do!"

The little man said nothing and went away, but a few
minutes later the eldest son tripped over a log and hurt
his ankle. He hobbled home, unable to finish his work.

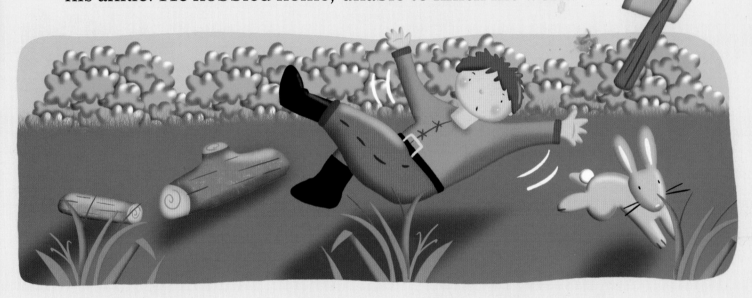

The next day, he still couldn't walk, so the middle son went
to the forest instead. He had cakes and milk for *his* lunch, too.

No sooner had the middle son sat down at lunchtime than
the little man appeared. "I'm hungry and thirsty," he said.
"Could I have a cake and some milk?"

"No!" said the middle son.
"Why should I give you *my* food?"

Once again, the little man went away, but a few minutes later, a branch fell on the middle son's shoulder, and he was not able to carry on working that day or the next.

"I'll go instead!" said the youngest son. Everyone laughed. "You'd be hopeless!" they jeered, but he was determined. His mother gave him some stale bread and water.

After a morning's work, the youngest son sat down to eat. At once, the little man appeared. "I'm hungry and thirsty," he said. "Could I have a cake and some milk?"

"I'm sorry, I don't have any," replied the youngest son, "but you can share my bread and water if you like."

After they had finished eating, the little man said, "You deserve a reward. Chop down that tree over there to find it."

With that, the little man disappeared, never to be seen again.

The youngest son set to work to cut down the tree.
As it fell, he saw that the trunk was hollow, and inside
was a goose, with feathers of pure gold.

Tucking the goose under his arm,
the youngest son decided not to go
home, where he was not wanted,
but to set off into the wide world.

"My golden goose will make me
rich and famous," he said to himself.

And it did.

The Other Frog Prince

One evening, as the stars began to shine, Mother Frog read her froglets the story of the Frog Prince.

"The Princess kissed the frog," she told her three children, "and at once he turned into a handsome Prince. The Prince and the Princess were married and lived happily ever after."

Young Fiona Frog sighed contentedly and went to sleep.
Little Freddie Frog giggled and settled down on his lily
pad. But Felix Frog was too excited to sleep. There and
then, he decided he would find a beautiful Princess,
turn into a handsome Prince, and marry her.

As soon as he was old enough, Felix set out to make his dream come true. He said goodbye to his mother, his sister and his brother and set off to find his Princess.
He hopped across fields…

paddled through puddles…

and swam across rivers…

until one day, in the distance, he saw a magnificent castle.
It had towers and turrets. Its flags and banners were
covered with flowers, and its walls were pink.

"That," said Felix to himself,
"is certainly the home of a beautiful Princess."

When he reached the castle, Felix found it was surrounded by wonderful gardens, and there, sitting under a flowering tree, was a Princess. She was certainly beautiful, but she looked bored and unhappy.

"She looks sad because she hasn't met me yet," said Felix to himself. He knew it might be difficult to persuade the Princess that he was really a Prince in disguise, so he hopped into a flowerbed and made himself a little crown from a golden flower.

Felix approached the Princess. He saw that she was holding a small picture of a young man. From time to time, she leaned down and kissed it with tears in her eyes.

Now Felix knew what to do. Instead of persuading the Princess to kiss him, he simply hopped on to the picture and waited. Sure enough, the Princess sighed, puckered up her lips and leaned down.

"Eeeeeuuuurgh!" She flung the picture from her. *"Help! Eeeeeeuuuurgh!* A dirty frog is on my picture of Prince Goodheart!" she shrieked.

Just then, the young man in the picture hurtled through a nearby hedge and swept the Princess up into his arms.

"I will save you, beloved!" he cried. "Forgive me for taking so long to return. I had trouble with my carriage."

While the Princess kissed her Prince, Felix hopped hurriedly away. His dreams were shattered. When he saw a pool of cool, shimmering water before him, he dived in with relief. He began to feel more like himself again.

A silvery voice interrupted him. "You've lost your crown, your Highness," said a charming young girl-frog, who was sitting on a lily leaf. She was holding his flower crown and wearing something similar herself.

"I'm … I'm not a Prince," stammered Felix, "not really."

"I'm not a Princess," smiled the new frog kindly, "but it's nice to pretend, isn't it?"

Felix had never been good with words. He thought of himself more as an action frog. But at that moment, the pretty girl-frog's sparkling eyes inspired him to say, "You're certainly pretty enough to be a Princess!"

The end of this story is easy to tell. The Princess kissed Felix and at once he became the handsome frog of her dreams. The Frog Princess and her Frog Prince were married and lived happily ever after.

The Enormous Turnip

Once upon a time, an old man and an old woman lived in a little cottage with a big garden. The old man loved to grow vegetables, and the old woman loved to cook them. They *both* loved to eat them!

One sunny morning in spring, the old man pulled on his gardening boots and went outside to plant some seeds. He had already prepared the soil, so it did not take him long to sprinkle the tiny seeds in careful rows.

"We'll soon have some tasty turnips to eat," he told his wife.

"I can't wait!" said the old woman.

Over the next few days, the sun shone and gentle rain fell on the garden. Before long, tiny green shoots could be seen above the ground. The shoots became small, green turnip leaves. Each day, they grew a little more, and under the soil, the turnip roots grew as well.

Before long, the young turnips were big enough to eat. The old man gathered a few each day, but one turnip seemed to be growing faster than the others.

"I'm going to leave that one," the old man told his wife. "It might win a prize at the Fruit and Vegetable Show."

The old man took great care of his prize turnip. He gave it special fertilizer and watered it during dry spells.

The turnip grew and grew.

"I've never seen a turnip like it," said the old man. "I'll pull it up the day before the show. It will take ages to clean up a vast vegetable like that."

Still the turnip grew. The old man began to wonder if it would fit in his wheelbarrow.

The morning came at last when the old man went out to pull up the turnip. It was so big, he didn't have to bend to grasp the leaves. Taking a firm hold, he leaned back and *pulled*.

The turnip didn't budge. The old woman was watching from the window. She hurried out to help her husband.

"One, two, three, *pull!*" shouted the old man. But the turnip didn't move.

The old man and the old woman heaved until they were exhausted. It was no good.

Just then, a boy came strolling along the lane at the bottom of the garden.

"Will you come and help us pull up this enormous turnip?" called the old man.

"Easy!" replied the boy. He jumped over the fence and held on to the old woman.

"One, two, three, *pull!*" shouted the old woman.

The old man, the old woman and the boy *pulled* with all their might. But they could not budge the turnip.

A girl came past on her way to school.

"Will you come and help us pull up this enormous turnip?" called the old man.

"One, two, three, *pull!*" cried the boy.

The old man, the old woman, the boy and the girl *pulled*. It was no good.

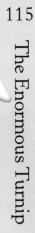

The boy spotted a dog in the meadow. He whistled, and the dog came bounding over to help.

"Careful!" said the girl, as the dog got hold of her skirt with his mouth. "One, two, three, *pull!*"

The old man, the old woman, the boy, the girl and the dog *pulled*. The turnip stayed stuck.

"Here, Puss!" called the girl, seeing a cat walking along the fence.

Down jumped the cat and took hold of the dog's tail.

"Woof, woof, woof, *woof!*" barked the dog.

The old man, the old woman, the boy, the girl, the dog and the cat *pulled.* It was hopeless.

Just then, the cat spotted a little mouse who had been watching right from the beginning. The little mouse scampered forward and took hold of the cat's tail.

"Meeow, meeow, meeow, *meeow!*" cried the cat, and everyone understood what *that* meant!

The old man, the old woman, the boy, the girl, the dog, the cat and the mouse *pulled* … and all of a sudden, the turnip popped out of the ground and everyone went flying.

Now everyone could see that it was the most enormous turnip that had ever been grown.

Of course, the turnip won top prize at the show. Afterwards, the old man, the old woman, the boy, the girl, the dog, the cat *and* the mouse sat down together to eat it. They all agreed: it was *enormously* delicious!

Moon Magic

O ver the hills and far away, in the middle of a forest, there lived an owl family. They were Father Owl, Mother Owl and Little Egg. A hole in a mighty oak tree was their home.

During the day, the owls slept, hidden from sight. At night, when the moon rose in the sky and the stars sparkled above, Father Owl and Mother Owl flew out of their home on silent wings. They swooped through the forest, looking for food.

Little Egg didn't swoop. He was safe in his shell, in a bed of feathers, in the hole, in the oak tree, in the forest.

One day, as spring slowly became summer in the woodland, the Mother Owl could hear a tiny calling sound from Little Egg. It was time for him to hatch. That night, Little Egg gently cracked open and someone very fluffy came out.

"Whoooo is this?" asked Father Owl, looking down at the bundle of fluff.

"It is Little Owl," said Mother Owl. "He is here at last."

Little Owl was snug and safe in his bed of feathers, in the hole, in the oak tree, in the forest.

Each night, Father Owl
and Mother Owl flew off
to find food for them all.

When he was all alone, Little Owl began to be worried.
He shuffled to the edge of the hole and looked up at the sky.
Something big and round was shining down at him. "Oooooo!"
said Little Owl.

When Mother Owl came home, he told her how the large shiny thing
in the sky had scared him. Mother Owl hooted with laughter. "It's
the moooooon," she said. "It is magic. Each night,
it shines down and keeps owls safe. When I'm
not here, the moon will look after you."

Little Owl was getting older now. He did a lot of thinking about things. After a few days, he found something new to worry about. He noticed that the moon was beginning to disappear. At first, he wasn't sure, but after a while he saw that each night there was a little bit less of the moon.

He wasn't sure if there was enough moon left to keep him safe each night.

Night by night, the moon got smaller and smaller, until it was just a silver sliver in the sky.

That night, Little Owl begged his mother not to go out.

"I have to go, Little Owl," she said, "or you will be hungry. You know that the magic moon will look after you."

"It isn't magic," said Little Owl sadly. "Something has been nibbling away at it. Last night there was hardly any moon. Tonight it won't be there at all."

"Nooooooo, Little Owl," smiled his mother. "That's why the moon is magic. Each month, it gets smaller and smaller night after night, until it is a tiny sliver. Then it begins to grow again, until one night it is big and round once more."

Little Owl wasn't sure, but he knew that his mother was very wise. Sure enough, over the next few nights the moon began to grow.

By the time the magic moon was big again, Little Owl was quite big, too. He understood lots of things now. Safe on a branch, near the hole, in the oak tree, in the forest, he smiled at the moon. And the moon smiled back.